Fairy Cornbread

WRITTEN BY ARIAN T. MOORE

To my family—You are my everything.

ISBN 978-0-578-76907-3

Library of Congress Control Number: 2020918239

Published by Eagle Nose Publishing.

Illustrated by Aria Jones
Co-Illustrated by Colin Moore

10 9 8 7 6 4 5 3 2 1

Tomorrow was Zoe's sixth birthday and she could hardly wait to have pink cupcakes with glittery gold sprinkles, a bounce house, face painting, and pony rides.

Zoe sat daydreaming about her party while eating dinner at Nana's house. Nana made some of Zoe's favorites; there was baked chicken, candied yams, green beans, and a choice of dinner rolls or Nana's famous cornbread. Zoe was the only one who chose cornbread. For some reason, to Zoe the cornbread looked like it was glowing.

"Nana, this cornbread is so so good," Zoe said. "I tried a little something different this time," Nana said. "I used a fairy blend of edible flowers and special spices."

Zoe felt a tickle on her hand and a tingle on her back. She ran to Nana's room to look in the mirror.

"Oh my gosh!" Zoe said. She had fairy wings on her back and a shimmering wand in her hand.

Hiding the wings in her shirt, she ran to the kitchen, hid the wand in a gift bag, and stuffed the rest of the fairy cornbread in her pocket.

"Alright guys, say thank you to Nana for dinner," Dad said. They said their goodbyes, and Zoe's dad grabbed the gift bag and drove them all home.

While putting on her favorite pink PJs, Zoe noticed that her wings had disappeared. "Thank goodness," she said. "How would I explain fairy wings to Mommy and Daddy?" She checked the gift bag from Nana; the magic wand had disappeared too.

After reading a book and saying prayers,
Zoe's mom sent her brothers to their
rooms with hugs and hi-fives, then tucked
Zoe in her bed and gave her a big hug.

"You are super loved and super special, Zoe's mom said, placing a pink bonnet on Zoe's head. "Now get some sleep so you'll have plenty of energy for all the fun tomorrow," her mom said.

"Good night, Mommy. But don't forget about the pink cupcakes with glittery gold sprinkles," Zoe said. "Well, honey," said Mom, "there was only vanilla icing and rainbow sprinkles at the store. I'm sure they will taste yummy."

"What about the Baby Like Me Doll for Piper?" Zoe asked. "Remember, I wanted to do something special for her since she didn't have a birthday party this year. She's been so sad since her mommy passed away."

"Oh no! I totally forgot," Zoe's mom said. "I had so much to do with the project at work, your brother's soccer game, and preparing for your party. I'm so sorry. We'll do something nice for Piper soon. Okay honey?"

"Okay," Zoe said slowly.

Zoe wasn't sad for long. I can fix this problem, easy peasy, she thought to herself, remembering the fairy cornbread she had stuffed in her pocket. She was too excited to sleep. "Happy birthday to me, happy birthday to me, I'm a princess . . . and a fairy, happy birthday to me," she sang to herself.

"Shhhhh! Go to sleep," her brothers Austin and Bradley said in unison.

Zoe closed her eyes and pretended
to be asleep . . . for a while.

When it was quiet, she peeked into her brothers' rooms to make sure they were asleep, tiptoed past her mom and dad's room, and ran down to the kitchen.

Zoe pulled out the leftover fairy cornbread and took a small bite. She felt a tickle on her hand and a tingle on her back.

With her fairy wings and her sparkly wand in tow, she took down the vanilla icing and rainbow sprinkles from the cabinet, waved her wand, and just like that she had perfectly baked cupcakes with pretty pink icing and glittery gold sprinkles. The kitchen was shimmering pink, sparkling gold, and the sweet aroma of cupcakes filled the air.

"Just what I wanted," Zoe said.

Another flick of her wand and the Baby Like Me Doll appeared on the counter, wrapped in a pink box and bow.

She had no idea that her brother Colin was wide awake and saw her fairy wings and sparkly wand. He even saw the present and the cupcakes that magically appeared on the counter.

Tired, Zoe flew back to her room and swiftly fell asleep.

The next morning, Zoe jumped up,
brushed her teeth, got dressed, made
her bed, and ran downstairs.

"Happy Birthday, Zoe!" the family sang.
"Thanks guys," she said.
"Ummmm... Zoe, what's that on your head?"
her brother Bradley asked.
"Are you supposed to be a chef?" her brother
Austin questioned.

Huh?," she said, patting her head. "Oh. I forgot to take it off. It's my new bonnet," Zoe explained, removing it. "Mommy said it will protect my hair and keep my puffs neat while I sleep."

Her dad placed a tiara on her head, picked her up on his shoulders, and gave her a ride through the living room. "Wheeee," Zoe squealed, smiling from ear to ear.

"I love you, baby girl," he said, gently placing her in her seat and kissing her on the forehead.

"How was your night, Zoe?" her mom asked.
"It was fantastic," Zoe said smiling at the strawberry pancakes still steaming from the griddle. She waited patiently for her three brothers to pass the syrup.

"The weirdest thing happened," her mom began to explain. "I came downstairs this morning and there, sitting on the counter, were pink cupcakes with glittery gold sprinkles and a perfectly wrapped pink present."

"Hmmm, that's a terrific, super, awesome mystery," Zoe said.

"Yeah, a mystery alright," her brother Colin said sarcastically. But he didn't tell the secret.

Later that afternoon, Zoe's Mom was putting the final touches on the party table when . . . Ding! Dong! The doorbell rang. It was Piper. "I love your hair," Piper said, admiring Zoe's puffs.

Zoe and Piper hugged and ran to the backyard to get a head start on the fun. They went straight for the castle bounce house.

As more guests arrived, Zoe's dad was finishing up on the grill and jamming to old school hits. Her mom and Nana were doing the Electric Slide.

After getting their faces painted, the younger children meandered from bounce house to bounce house. The older children started a casual game of basketball.

"Time to sing Happy Birthday," Zoe's mom said. After they sang, Zoe blew out her candles. Her mom, singing the Stevie Wonder version of the birthday song, passed out the glittery cupcakes.

Zoe had a wonderful time with her friends and brothers. The cupcakes were a hit, and they were so delicious. Pink icing with glittery gold sprinkles, just like she wanted.

As Piper grabbed her party bag, Zoe stopped her. "Wait, I have something for you." Zoe gave Piper the present with a big grin. "Happy belated birthday, Piper."

"Piper was so happy; she swiftly unwrapped the present. "A Baby Like Me Doll? Thank you, Zoe," she said, jumping up and down. "You're welcome," Zoe said. They hugged and Piper said goodbye.

While her mom and dad were busy
cleaning, Zoe and Colin were alone in the
living room. Colin was reading, and Zoe
was playing with her doll house.
"So, Zoe, for my birthday, think you can
turn that homemade cake Mommy makes
into a warrior cake?" Colin asked.

She dropped her doll and looked at him in a
panic. He had such a serious look on his face,
she didn't know what to think.
Then he came over, tickled and hugged her, and
said, "Okay, okay . . . a ninja cake will do."
They both laughed.

"Hey guys, your aunt and uncle are coming down from D.C., next week, so we'll have dinner at Nana's again on Sunday," Zoe's mom said.

"Oh, great, Mommy," Zoe said. "But whatever you do, don't eat the cornbread."

CPSIA information can be obtained
at www.ICGtesting.com
Printed in the USA
BVHW020956271220
596498BV00024B/342